Zachary Zebra's Zippity Zooming

by Barbara deRubertis • illustrated by R.W. Alley

THE KANE PRESS / NEW YORK

Alpha Betty's Class

Nina Nandu

Oliver Otter

Polly Porcupine

Quentin Quokka

Rosie Raccoon

Sammy Skunk

Tessa Tiger

Umma Ungka

Victor Vicuna

Walter Warthog

Xavier Ox

Yoko Yak

Zachary Zebra

STAR of the BOOK

Alpha Betty

Library of Congress Cataloging-in-Publication Data

deRubertis, Barbara.
Zachary Zebra's zippity zooming / by Barbara deRubertis ; illustrated by R.W. Alley.
p. cm. — (Animal antics A to Z)
Summary: Zachary Zebra has had a blitz of bad luck, but after his concerned teacher,
Alpha Betty, asks if he is getting enough sleep and a good breakfast,
he makes a change that brings back his zippity zoom.
ISBN 978-1-57565-359-4 (library binding : alk. paper) — ISBN 978-1-57565-351-8 (pbk. : alk. paper) —
ISBN 978-1-57565-390-7 (e-book)
[1. Sleep—Fiction. 2. Food habits—Fiction. 3. Zebras—Fiction. 4. Animals—Fiction. 5. Alphabet.]
I. Alley, R. W. (Robert W.), ill. II. Title.
PZ7.D4475Zac 2011
[E]—dc22   2010051474

1 3 5 7 9 10 8 6 4 2

First published in the United States of America in 2011 by Kane Press, Inc.
Printed in the United States of America
WOZ0711

Series Editor: Juliana Hanford
Book Design: Edward Miller

Animal Antics A to Z is a registered trademark of Kane Press, Inc.

www.kanepress.com

The sun was blazing in the window.
The alarm clock was buzzing.
But Zachary Zebra was still snoozing.

Dad nuzzled Zachary's neck.
Zachary snoozed on.

Dad began singing a jazzy wake-up song.
Zachary snoozed on.

Dad slowly pulled off Zachary's cozy covers.
"Help! I'm freezing!" Zachary fussed.

Dad laughed. "What happened to our zippity zooming zebra? I think he went away . . . and a lazybones zebra took his place!"

Zachary grumbled as he sat down for breakfast.
"My brain is fuzzy. My eyes are snoozy.
And I'm not hungry."

"Are you sick?" asked Mom.

"No," said Zachary. "But I don't want to
go to school."

Mom and Dad looked puzzled.
"You love Alpha Betty's school!" said Dad.

"What's wrong, Zachary?" asked Mom.

"Oh, nothing," said Zachary.
But then words tumbled out of his mouth.

"On Monday, we had a math quiz.
I didn't get *any* answers right.
Zero. Zip. Zilch.

On Tuesday, we ran races during recess.
I kept falling down. I felt like such a klutz.

Yesterday during lunch, I sneezed.
I dropped my zucchini pizza on the floor.
And zucchini pizza is my favorite!

Alpha Betty said I was having a blitz of
bad luck."

"You've had a doozie of a week!" said Mom.

"You need a blitz of GOOD luck!" said Dad.
"We need to have our zippity zooming zebra back!"

"I don't know why my zippity zooming fizzled out,"
said Zachary. "I'll have to think about it."

Zachary zipped up his fuzzy jacket.
And he stumbled off to school.

Zachary squeezed through the door just as the
bell rang.
"Are you okay, Zachary?" whispered Alpha Betty.
"You look a little frazzled today."

"I'm okay . . . I guess," said Zachary.

During math, Zachary's tummy buzzed and
grumbled.
"Did you eat a good breakfast?" Alpha Betty
whispered to Zachary.

"Not exactly," Zachary said.

During story time, Zachary dozed off to sleep.
"Are you getting enough sleep?" Alpha Betty
whispered to Zachary later.

"Well . . . ," said Zachary.

That night Dad fixed zucchini pizza for dinner.

"Did you figure out why your zippity zooming fizzled out?" Mom asked Zachary.

"I do have ONE idea," Zachary said.

When it was bedtime, Zachary did some things differently.

As usual, Mom and Dad read Zachary a story. They kissed him good night. They turned off the light. And they closed the door.

But this time, Zachary did NOT turn the light back on.

And he did NOT stay up late reading one of his super-scary Zoey Zombie books!

ZOEY ZOMBIE

The next morning, Zachary's alarm buzzed.

When Dad opened the door, Zachary was
already dressed. And he was looking GOOD!

Zachary *zipped* downstairs.

He ate a big bowl of oatmeal with frozen bananas.

He ran outside and picked a bouquet of zinnias.

And then he *zoomed* off to school!

Mom and Dad were amazed!

Alpha Betty was also amazed when Zachary arrived
at school *early* . . . and gave her the zinnias.
"Thank you, Zachary!" said Alpha Betty.
"You look snazzy today!"

Zachary gave Alpha Betty a dazzling smile.

First, there was a math quiz.

"I am a math whiz!" Zachary said to himself.

He blazed through the quiz.

And he got all the answers right!

During recess, Zachary ran races.
He zigzaggèd around the rocks.
He zippity zoomed between the trees.
Zachary was full of pizzazz!

After lunch, the class held their weekly Crazy
Cap Club meeting. They ate dozens of cookies.
And Alpha Betty read zany stories about
a lazy lizard and a dizzy grizzly.

Zachary did NOT doze off!

Soon it was time to go home.
Zachary zipped up his fuzzy jacket.

"Today you had a blitz of GOOD luck,
Zachary!" said Alpha Betty.
"Whatever it is you're doing, keep it up!"

Zachary zippity zoomed all the way home.

He gave Mom and Dad a dazzling smile.
"Your zippity zooming zebra is BACK!"
he said proudly.

When it was time for bed, Mom and Dad read Zachary a story. They kissed him good night. They turned off the light. They closed the door.

ZOEY ZOMBIE

And Zachary turned the light back on!
"Tomorrow is Saturday," he grinned.
"I can sleep late!"

Zachary picked up a super-scary Zoey Zombie book.
He opened it. . . . But then he closed it again.

Zachary laughed. "I'll read this when it's daylight,"
he said.

Then he picked up a book of bedtime stories.

And after a while, the only sound from Zachary Zebra's room was, "**Zzzzzzzzzzzzzz!**"

FUN FACTS

- Home: Most of the three surviving species of zebras live on the African plains or on rocky mountain hillsides, south of the Sahara Desert.
- Family: Zebras travel in family groups led by a stallion, with as many as 200,000 zebras in a herd! If young zebras wander off for a while, their parents will find them again!
- Appearance: Each zebra has its own unique pattern of black or brown stripes. Like a fingerprint, it is unlike the stripe pattern on any other zebra! Zebras have a heavy head, stout body, stiff mane, and tufted tail.
- Favorite foods: Zebras primarily eat grass.
- **Did You Know?** Zebras are VERY fast runners, sometimes reaching speeds of nearly 40 miles per hour!

LOOK BACK

Learning to identify letter sounds (phonemes) at the beginning, middle, and end of words is called "phonemic awareness."

- The word *zip* begins with the z sound. Listen to the words on page 24 being read again. When you hear a word that begins with the z sound, repeat the word and extend the zzzzz sound (zzzzz*ip*)!
- The word *buzzer* has the z sound in the middle. Listen to the words on page 25 being read again. When you hear a word that has the z sound in the middle, repeat the word and extend the zzzzz sound (*bu*zzzzz*er*)!

TRY THIS!

Read Zany Words with Zachary Zebra!

- Fold a piece of paper in half to make a "book". *
- Write the following silly words in a list on the left inside "page" of the book: zap, zep, zip, zop, zup.
- Write these silly words in a list on the right page: fazz, fezz, fizz, fozz, fuzz.
- Now read each word by blending the sounds together. If it's a real word, tell what it means. If it's not a real word, make up a definition!

* A printable, ready-to-use copy of this "book" is available at Zachary's website: www.kanepress.com/AnimalAntics/ZacharyZebra.html

FOR MORE ACTIVITIES, go to Zachary Zebra's website: www.kanepress.com/AnimalAntics/ZacharyZebra.h
You'll also find a recipe for Zachary Zebra's Zippy Zucchini Boats!